HERE AND THEN

A Richard Jackson Book

Also by the Author

Borrowed Children
Red Rover, Red Rover

To ,

for remembering.

1994

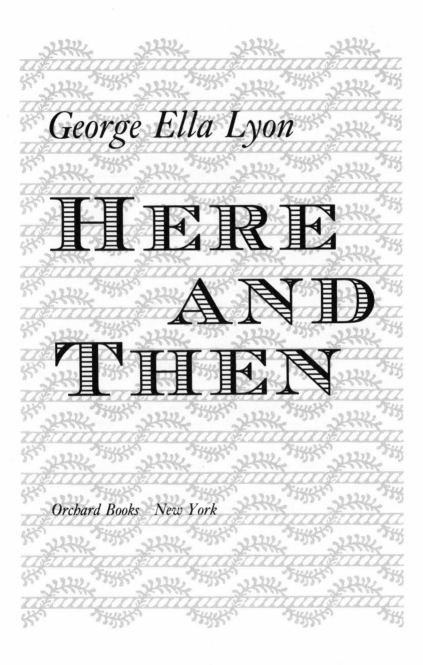

George Ella Lyon

HERE AND THEN

Orchard Books   New York

Orchard Books, 95 Madison Avenue, New York, NY 10016

Manufactured in the United States of America
Book design by Mina Greenstein
The text of this book is set in 12 point Janson.
1 3 5 7 9 10 8 6 4 2

Library of Congress Cataloging-in-Publication Data
Lyon, George Ella, date.
Here and then / George Ella Lyon.
p. cm. "A Richard Jackson book"—Half t.p.
Summary: Through ghostly visitation and a diary that seems
mysteriously to write itself with twelve-year-old Abby's hands,
a Civil War nurse asks for help with medical supplies across an
abyss of 133 years.
ISBN 0-531-06866-8. ISBN 0-531-08716-6 (lib. bdg.)
[1. Supernatural—Fiction. 2. United States—History—
Civil War, 1861–1865—Fiction. 3. Nurses—
Fiction.] I. Title. PZ7.L9954He 1994
[Fic]—dc20 94-6921

ACKNOWLEDGMENTS

The author wishes to thank

SUSAN LYONS HUGHES of the Kentucky Historical Society for sharing her knowledge of the time and place, her resources, and her experience as a Civil War reenactor;

PAT BALLARD of the Garrard County Historical Society for materials about the Hoskins family and Hoskins Crossroads; and

JANIE GRACE ROBINSON, great-niece of Eliza Hoskins, for sharing her memories and family history.

For PAUL CANTRELL

For HARPER

and the times

we have traveled

I hope I have God on my side,
but I must have Kentucky.

—ABRAHAM LINCOLN

O N E

I KEEP DREAMING the house. Moonlight maps the upstairs floor, littered with leaves and plaster. I dream I am in my sleeping bag near the window, campfires below it like low stars. My parents are asleep down there in one of the tents pitched by the reenactors. In Civil War nightshirt and nightdress they're pretending to be a long-dead couple.

Others are still up, singing. Their song reaches me:

> The years creep slowly by, Lorena.
> The snow is on the ground again.
> The sun's low down the sky, Lorena.
> The frost gleams where the flowers have been.
> But the heart beats on as warmly now
> As when the summer days were nigh. . . .

The old house is hot, the air close. I get up, slip out of the room and down a narrow hall, then reach for a door that leads to the upstairs porch. It opens in the dream, and I step out onto slanted floorboards. Because it's set into the house, the porch has a rail only across the front. There must have been chairs up here once, cane-bottom or wicker. Now it's empty. I stand at the rail and breathe September: corn stalks and tobacco drying, heavy heat.

No music out here, just the whicker of horses. Then a wind comes up. The trees creak. Plain old trees. How could I have thought there was life in this house? Thought the past lingered? Thought Eliza, whose part I played, was somehow speaking to me? Even in dream I can see my illusion. What I've camped out in for a weekend is a shell, like the cicada husks clinging to those trees.

The wind shifts, the wood strains, and it's not the trees I hear, it's the house, bowed out like a sail. With its white front silvered by the moon, the house comes loose and is launched, easy as a leaf. I stand at a ship's rail now, nightdress blowing. Never mind that I went to sleep in a Wildcat T-shirt, that the waves we ride are in fact Kentucky fields. . . .

THE UNDERTOW of this dream drags me out, but I struggle against it, willing myself up into air and light.

That's it, I think, lying out of breath on my own pillow. I can't keep this to myself anymore. No matter how stupid it sounds, I've got to tell Harper. She's not under the influence of re-enactors. She'll know what to do.

I get up, pull on shorts and a shirt, and head for the bathroom. Then downstairs to face break-fast and the first day of seventh grade.

T W O

FINALLY IT'S FOUR O'CLOCK. Harper and I are sitting on my bed. We've microwaved some nachos and carried up Cokes, and I'm going to begin this story. If there's sense in here somewhere, Harper will find it. If there's not, she'll keep it a secret.

"Dive in," she says, popping the can top.

"Okay," I say, doing the same. We laugh. Last year that was the sign of our friendship—popping the tops together and exchanging the rings.

[4]

We both take a drink, and I begin.

"Over Labor Day I wrote the diary of a woman dead eighty years."

"*What?*" Harper asks.

"You don't like that? How about this? I went away for the weekend to 1861."

"You went thirty miles to where grown-ups play Civil War," she counters.

"True. And somebody there offered me a job."

"You? You're only twelve."

I take a deep breath and look Harper straight in the eyes.

"She's a nurse. Back then. She needs help."

"You don't expect me to believe that, Abby," Harper says. "You don't even sound like yourself. You've been with a bunch of grown-ups who spend their free time dressing up as dead people and then pretending to kill each other. That could make you believe anything."

"It's not about believing," I tell her.

"What?" she asks again.

"Think about it. I've thought and thought, ever since we got back last night. Do you believe what happens to *you*?"

"Sure. Well, mostly," she says.

"And what if you don't?"

[5]

"Huh?"

"Like if your house is on fire and you can't believe it, will it stop burning?"

"Of course not. But—"

"No. It goes right on happening. It doesn't matter if you believe it. It just is."

"I don't know what you're talking about, Abby, and you're giving me the creeps. Is this something you learned at drama camp?" Harper asks.

"No. But it's because of drama camp Mom was able to talk me into going to the reenactment in the first place."

"I wondered about that. You always stayed at my house before."

"Yeah, but Mom said it would be good experience, and Ms. Consuelo, my drama coach at camp, said take any role you can get, so—"

"Okay, okay," Harper interrupts. "Don't give me the whole history. What happened?"

"I'm coming to it. See, Ms. Consuelo told us one way to get into a character is to keep a diary for her, and when Mom wanted me to take the part of an actual person, this nurse named Eliza Hoskins, well, I thought it would be kind of neat to try that. . . ." Saying this makes my skin crawl. I do the wet-dog shake.

"Not so neat, huh?" Harper says.

"You got it."

"Why not?"

"It worked."

Harper's not the kind to get the shivers, but I can tell this bothers her because she climbs off the bed and starts doing knee bends. After about ten, she says, "Who was this person?"

"They called her the Angel of Camp Robinson. A forty-year-old woman."

"Wasn't there a kid's part you could play?" Harper asks.

"They were having a war. They didn't bring their kids. Anyway, Miss Eliza lived in the house beside the training camp. It was on her family's land. And when the soldiers started to get sick—"

"You mean wounded," Harper breaks in.

"No, I don't. And if you keep interrupting, I'll never get this told." I take a deep breath, remembering *her* parents don't talk Civil War every night.

"Okay. Don't bite my head off," she says, crunching a tortilla chip.

"A lot more soldiers died of disease than died from battle," I tell her. "At Camp Robinson, where we were, where Miss Eliza was, the trouble was measles. It was at the start of the war, and the men were crowded together without enough food or supplies. Or enough clothes. When so many got sick, the camp doctor panicked. They weren't even fighting yet, and he couldn't tend them all. That's when the Angel stepped in. She

[7]

became a nurse to the men in the field and took some of the sickest into her house."

"Wasn't she afraid of getting sick, too?" Harper asks.

"I don't think so. Not from what she writes."

"Writes?"

"Harper, I am getting to that. Will you be quiet?"

She nods.

"If you keep stopping me, I'll get lost, and I'm lost enough as it is."

She crosses her heart. I think she thinks I'm kidding. "Go on," she says.

"That's almost all they know about Eliza. When the epidemic was over and the first bunch of troops moved out, she went on nursing whoever came to the camp. They could be sick or wounded, Union or Rebel—it didn't matter to her. And after the war, she married and lived out her life in that house."

"So what's the big deal?" Harper asks, forgetting her promise.

"She's still there," I say, digging the diary out of my backpack, fluttering the pages to show it's almost full.

Harper looks blank.

"This weekend I did what Ms. Consuelo said and tried to keep a diary for Eliza. I wrote all these pages. See? It's my handwriting"—Harper takes the notebook—"but it's not my words. *She* wrote it, Harper, fast and furious, like she'd been waiting for someone to give her the chance to speak."

Harper flips a few pages, then opens the notebook and reads:

muslin
kettle
cups
tent canvas
whiskey
salve for powder burns

Some complain of their ears, and I have run out of sweet oil. I sponge their faces and hands. Yesterday a boy, delirious, cried, "Jane! Jane!" and I replied, God help me, "Here I am." He clutched my hand, smiled, and tried to sit up. Died with the homelight blazing in his face.

Harper shuts the diary and lays it on the bed, slowly, carefully, as though it might blow up.

"This better not be a joke, Abby," she says.

I shake my head.

"I wish it was," we both say at once, then laugh. But the sound is strange. It's like fear shook us so hard, a half laugh fell out.

"Are you going to tell anybody?" Harper asks.

"I can't yet," I say. "It's not over."

"What do you mean?"

Harper looks so secure sitting there, so "right now" in her jeans and Metallica sweatshirt. She's put her brown hair in dog ears like some little kid, and I think, Hey, is it fair to drag her into this?

Then I look at the notebook full of words written so hard they ripple the page: *You* must *listen*, Eliza wrote. *You were sent to me, the help I've been praying for.*

"Harper," I say, "there's something she wants us to do."

THREE

"ABBY," HARPER BEGINS, chewing on strands of her hair—a bad sign. "What if you've, like, lost your mind or something? You know, just temporarily."

"Do I look like I've lost my mind?"

"No, but—"

"Do I sound like it?"

She shakes her head. "But what you *say* sounds a little . . ."

"Crazy?"

She nods.

"I thought about that all night. But look." I pull up my shirtsleeve to show a cluster of red marks along my arm.

Harper looks alarmed. "You're getting their measles?"

It's tempting to say yes and hope that convinces her, but I'd better stick to the truth.

"That's where I pinched myself when I was writing," I tell her. "To make sure it was really me. But someone else was with me. And it wasn't *now*, Harper, it was *then*."

"How do you know?" she asks.

"I got up and went to the window once—"

"What window? I thought you were camping out."

"I was, but it was in Eliza's house. It's run-down and empty now, but they let the reenactors use it. Since I was being Eliza, that's where I slept. I even wore her clothes."

"Not her real clothes."

"Didn't I tell you that?"

"Later. Go back to the window," Harper orders.

"When I looked out, I saw the field, rows of tents, campfires—"

"But that was your parents!" she says.

"I thought so, too. Then I looked across the road, thinking, since I was upstairs, I could see where the cars were parked, down a hill, hidden from the camp. But there weren't any cars, there wasn't any *road*, paved road, I mean. No highway signs, telephone wires, power lines. And when I turned back to the room, the ratty wallpaper and the bare floor with my sleeping bag were gone. There was rosy carpet and a narrow bed spread with a pink-and-white quilt." I shiver, remembering.

"Did you see her?" Harper wants to know.

"No."

"Was there a mirror?"

I nod.

"Well?"

"I *couldn't* look in, Harper. I was too scared. I had on her clothes and everything—"

"But you might have been her!"

"Don't say that!" Like a dweeb, I start crying. Harper tries to hug me and knocks over the Coke I've forgotten to drink. I run to the bathroom for a towel. As if to make up for lost nerve, I glance in the mirror. It's me, all right: teary blue eyes behind glasses, round face, blond hair short and shiny.

"I believe you," Harper offers, as I come back in.

"That's good," I say, sponging up Coke from the bedspread, the floor.

"Nobody else will," she adds.

"I know. But they won't have to," I tell her. "I've got you."

"Let me see the clothes."

"Eliza's?"

Harper nods.

"Why?"

"I'm curious."

"Okay," I say, "but I'm not putting them on."

"Nobody asked you to. Don't be such a crab."

I go to the closet and take out Eliza's long brown skirt with tiers of tucks above the hem, her tea-dyed blouse with twenty tiny buttons. I lay them across Harper's lap as she sits on the bed.

"Sheesh!" she exclaims. "Imagine having to get through a war in this!" She lifts one sleeve of the blouse, then tosses it so the cuff rests at the collar. "Didn't it make you feel weird to wear it?"

"Special, maybe, the way costumes do. Not weird."

"Just put on the shirt."

"No, Harper. This isn't a game."

"Okay, then. I will."

And in five seconds she's stripped off her sweatshirt, taken the blouse off the hanger, and is poking her arms through the sleeves. I hold my breath. When she buttons it up, her whole body looks astonished.

"Whoa!" Harper says.

"What is it?"

"This thing makes my skin crawl." She gets out of it fast. "What's it made out of?"

"I don't know. Cotton, probably."

"Whatever it is, I don't like it."

"Maybe it's electricity."

"What?"

"Maybe it's like a current from her to us—"

"Stop it, Abby!"

"No, listen. The blouse makes you itchy because you resist the current. I take it in . . . and write in her voice."

I expect her to throw the wet towel at me, but she just stares, then tilts her head as if to get a different view.

"You're not kidding, are you?" she asks.

"No."

She heaves Eliza's clothes at me.

"Take this stuff back where it came from!"

The roughness in her voice means she might cry, which is not like Harper. I take my time slipping the skirt into the closet, rehanging the blouse. I give her a chance to get it together.

Finally she says, "So what is it Eliza wants us to do?"

FOUR

"BRING SUPPLIES," I tell her, turning around.

"You can't be serious."

"*She's* serious," I say.

"Like stuff on that list?"

I nod.

"How?"

"On the bus, I guess."

"Abby!" She jumps to her feet. "You *are* crazy!" She is pacing the little room. "You think we're going to get on a Greyhound bus with a kettle and some whiskey? We're going to get tickets to 1861?"

I flop onto the bed, pull my pillow over my face. "You can make anything sound stupid, Harper."

"This is not exactly hard," she says.

I lift the corner of the pillow and see she's standing on her toes, doing arm rotations.

"Okay. Forget it. I'll go by myself."

She bounds onto the bed. "That's not what I mean, Abby. Look, I have to be home in fifteen minutes. If you've got a plan, let's hear it."

I sit up, hugging the pillow. "You've still got your Girl Scout uniform?"

"What?" She's exasperated.

"*Do* you?"

"I think so. It's got to be too short."

"Never mind," I tell her. "Just bring it tomorrow. Tell your mom you have chorus or something after school. We're going to hit a new subdivision door-to-door for hurricane relief."

"Abby! That's lying! Or stealing or something—"

"No, it's not," I say in my most soothing voice. I've thought this through. "There *was* a bad hurricane in South Carolina last month. People want to help. And if this works, they *will* be helping. Just not helping who they think."

"Or *when*," Harper puts in.

"That's right."

"But, Abby—" Harper has to get up again. She's just got one energy level, like the eternal flame. She puts her foot against the wall between the desk and the bed and starts doing leg stretches. "Assuming we can get this money and we can get supplies and we do take a bus to this house of Eliza's, how are we going to get the stuff to her?"

"Dinner!" Mom calls up the stairs.

"Just a minute!" I yell back. I can smell the meat loaf and potatoes she's taken from the oven.

"I don't know," I tell Harper. "But Eliza must. We have to trust that. Maybe I can write to her in the journal and ask her to meet us."

Harper stops stretching. She straightens up and looks scared.

"Or maybe we can leave it there like an offering," I go on.

"We could get in a lot of trouble," she says.

"Yep."

"And if we tried explaining, people would think we're crazy."

"Yep."

"And you want to do it anyway?"

"No!" I say, surprised at how the blood rushes to my face. "I *don't* want to do it, Harper. I want to forget the whole thing. But I can't. It's like some door has opened, and I can't walk away. I can't close it. If we do this for Eliza, maybe she will."

"We don't have to go through the door?" Harper asks. She's perfectly still now.

"I don't think so."

"Abby!" It's Mom's voice again.

Harper grabs her books from the desk, and we start downstairs.

"Call me if you can't find your outfit, okay?" It's all I can think to say. Suddenly I feel like a balloon with its air whooshed out.

FIVE

DINNER IS NOT a problem. Mom serves the meat loaf. Dad asks about seventh grade.

"So far, so good," I tell him.

Mom wants to know about my teachers.

"Mr. Musick for Spanish, Mr. Clayton for social studies, Ms. Allen for English, Mrs. Whitaker for science, Ms. Yancey for math, and I-don't-know-who for study hall."

"I'm glad you have Nancy Allen," Mom says. "I've heard she's a great teacher."

I nod, though I've never heard that. Great for parents?

"Would you pass the sour cream?" Dad asks. This is a joke.

"If there was any in the house, I certainly would," Mom answers.

"And if she didn't love you, she'd buy some,"

I say, completing the ritual. Then I pass Dad the tub of I Can't Believe It's Not Butter!

"I can't believe it's not sour cream," he says, helping himself to a dollop. Then he carefully mashes and scrapes till the yellow is mixed with every bite of the potato. That's my dad, very thorough.

"So why aren't you taking history?" he asks.

"It's part of social studies," I tell him.

Mom gives me a now-you've-said-it look.

"History," Dad proclaims, "is not *part* of anything. Everything is part of history. If people would just pay attention to that—"

"I know," Mom says, trying to short-circuit the lecture. "It would be a much better world."

"Not for me," I say. "I'd have to take history *and* geography and lose my study hall."

They laugh and start dredging up their memories of seventh grade. I smile and nod when they need me to, but I'm thinking about tomorrow. I'm relieved when dinner is over so I can load the dishwasher and head upstairs.

I rush through homework, take a bath. Then I rummage through the recycling and get a coffee can to put our donations in. I tell Mom it's needed at school for dry markers. I explain how Jesse

Bancroft used the wrong kind in English, and Ms. Allen had him clean it off with fingernail-polish remover, which gave everybody up front a headache. So we need to keep the markers separate. This is true.

I cut a label from shelf paper, make the sign, and tape it to the can. Then I cut a slot in the plastic lid (salvaged from the cabinet of plastic things), and it's done. I get into bed, read till I'm sleepy, turn out the light.

It's the dark that does it.

The only thing I can see are the red numbers on my alarm clock. I'm glad they're there. There was no electricity at Camp Robinson so I didn't take a clock. Besides, I had the bugle to wake me.

"No bugles, no soldiers, no war"—I'm actually saying this under my breath when the door opens, the door from the hall, *our* hall, which has the laundry hamper, the bookcase full of Civil War books. I see a little light, glowing round as if from a candle, move across to my desk. Nothing else. I don't see or hear a person. I feel her presence, though, the way you know in your shoulders when someone's standing behind you.

Eliza? I feel myself try to speak but don't know if there's sound or only a pain in my throat. I shrink down into the bed. I close my eyes and try to will her away. Go back! I say to her in my head. You don't belong here! I've got my hands over my ears, my eyes squeezed shut. But, like a four-year-old pressing against a door a grown-up wants to open, I feel myself giving, sliding back where I don't want to go.

I see myself get out of bed and move to the desk like a moth to the light. Eliza's set the candle there. As I sit down, the flame jumps with my breath. I pick up the pen. My heart beats a full march, louder than the chair creaking, the fumble for the diary, the airplane roaring overhead. The pen moves jerkily, like a pulse.

> *In the beginning my fears were all prophetic. Before I stood in my apron stained like a butcher's and watched these boys cut apart. These boys who rode out as if to a picnic. Blasted like trees by lightning, laid open at the throat by the beast. Is right and wrong a part of this war? God, if I am to face another day, tell me where the right lies.*

I don't know I'm crying, yet tears spot the page. I'm blotting my eyes with a handkerchief. I will not look at it, not even at my hands.

I foresaw the flesh, red and swollen around the
wound, but not the horror of the wound itself. Any-
thing you can bring to ease or cover it—
We need shirts, shoes, bandages, chloroform. We need
meal, lard, flour, preserves. We need barber scissors,
pen and paper, ink, wine, soap, tooth powder, needle
and thread. Pillows, could anyone spare them. Aprons
of calico! Did I say coffee? Always more socks. Stamps
and a record book. I have filled two already with names
of those who have come here—where they started from,
where they are sent. It's my reckoning. And I say to
them, foolishly, I know, but sometimes it's all I can
give: "You'll not be forgotten. See: I have written your
name." No angel, I will be what I can.
Blankets we have need of. Potatoes—

And when the alarm goes off, I jerk awake at
my desk. For a minute I'm confused, then it all
comes back. I don't even have to read the diary. I
know what's there. In the mirror on the closet
door I find my face is wrinkled from sleeping all
night with my head on my arms. Looking closer,
I see a line of words transferred to my cheek. I
back away a little, and it looks like a scar.

What did I tell Harper? We would be disguised
as Girl Scouts? Put on uniforms? I see mine at the
back of the closet behind an old coat. I pull it out.

It's even got the badge sash, my scribe badge. I've always loved to write. This strikes me as hysterical, with Eliza's diary on the desk, tearstained, slept on. I start laughing so hard, Dad knocks on the door.

"You okay in there?" he asks.

"Yeah, Dad," I answer, my words jumping with the laughs.

"I'm out of the shower," he says. "The bathroom's yours."

"Thanks," I say, shaking my head, trying to get the laughing stopped. It sputters out in hiccups.

I close the diary, fold the uniform, put them both in my backpack. We'll see what happens, Harper. I don't think they have a badge for this.

SIX

SCHOOL GOES BY in slow motion. Math is long, life science is longer, social studies is forever. Harper says, at the lockers between classes, that even band lasted about a year.

"I know the feeling," I tell her, but as I walk on to Spanish I'm thinking, If an hour in the present was a year in the past, the war would be long over. I'm considering this when I come through a door and collide with Mr. Musick.

"¿Adonde vas, Ebe?" he asks. Every student's name has been españoled.

After the bell Mr. Musick explains that Wednesdays will be drill days. This means he will call on us seat by seat, row by row to translate vocabulary and conjugate verbs. Just for today we can use our books. It's not like a military drill, I tell myself while the kids do as ordered. It's not like soldiers in parallel formation, practicing orders to march or attack. We sit; our words rise and fall. When it's my turn, my answer is right apparently, for the questions keep moving. If Mr. Musick had a bugle, *una corneta*—I look this up—or a fife and drum, *un pífano y un tambor*, think how different this would be! What if *drill* meant Spanish students saluting and marching from *"Buenos días"* to *"Buenas noches"*? I can hear Mr. Musick now, "Hut, *dos*, *tres*, *cuatro*. . . ." The rest of the hour I have to follow along in the book to keep from laughing.

After a quick lunch with Harper—we share one order of pizza to save money for bus fare—I do health and study hall and that's it.

In study hall I've got my Spanish book open, my notebook ready, when it occurs to me: Didn't the Spanish have a civil war? I wonder what *that* was like. I flip through the book but can't find any history. The closest thing is a page about flags—*las banderas*—which declares: *La bandera de los Estados Unidos es roja, blanca, y azul*. Actually, in 1861, *both* sides had flags that were red, white, and blue. Why didn't the Confederates choose their own colors? It might have helped. . . .

Whoa! This isn't what I need to be studying. I need to focus on this afternoon. Assuming people do give us money, how much stuff can we take? What would be most important? How will we carry it? I've seen workers put boxes tied up with twine in the bus baggage compartment. Can we each take a suitcase and a box? How would we get out of our houses with suitcases? Well, we wouldn't. We'll have to have duffel bags, something that folds small. But one blanket would *fill* a duffel bag, and how are we going to get from the mall to the bus station with it?

Then it hits me: we won't go to the mall. We'll go downtown to the army surplus store. Army blankets are tight-woven and thin (now I see why), and we could get the tent canvas there, too, and maybe some other things she asked for. Plus there's a drugstore just across the street. All of this is close to a bus stop, and that will get us out to the station and on our way.

I think we should get bandages and peroxide, Bactine, general first-aid gear. I make lists. I make them in the diary, on the off chance that Eliza can read them. My concentration must look strange for study hall because Mrs. Ferguson taps me on the shoulder.

"Hard work for so early in the year, Abby," she tells me.

I nod. "I love history," I say, on an impulse.

Mrs. Ferguson glances at my open book, then leans down to look harder.

"But that's Spanish," she says.

"I know. I do the history in my head."

I can tell Mrs. Ferguson can't decide if I'm weird or rude. Finally she shrugs and walks away.

SEVEN

So HARPER AND I MEET in the Blue Wing bathroom after school to change clothes.

"If we hurry," she says, "we can catch the three-
fifteen bus." She knows the schedule because
that's how she gets to piano lessons.

"But if we do that," I warn her, "all the kids
waiting for school buses will see us in these out-
fits."

"No problem," Harper says. "I brought plastic
raincoats." She fishes them out, one pink, one
olive drab. "I know it's not raining. But if we put
up the hoods and run, no one will know who we
are, much less have time to ask questions."

"Okay." I speed up my clothes change. The
skirt is too short and too big in the waist. The
blouse barely buttons. Even if my breasts are

small, they're bigger than they were. That's something.

Harper's skirt looks as if it should be shorts. Luckily she's brought tights to wear with it. Nothing can be done about the sleeves of her blouse, though, two inches above her wrists.

"We look like Goodwill shoppers," Harper says.

Actually my folks get a lot of stuff at Goodwill, but I don't say so. It's my secret shame.

"Not really," I say. "There we'd get clothes that fit. We look more like refugees who had to take what someone handed out. Or soldiers. Come on."

We leave by the door at the end of Blue Wing, avoiding the school-bus crowd and the playground.

[*32*] We sling on our backpacks and run, plastic flapping, the two blocks to the bus stop. I watch the sidewalk fly beneath my feet. Some kid has painted a message on the bench at the bus stop: HOME WORK IS TWO FOUR-LETTER WORDS.

The bus pulls up right away.

Luck-y, Harper mouths.

"Yeah," I whisper, not sure why we're being secretive here. Practice maybe.

It's a ten-minute ride to Meadowbrook Chase, a new development south of the city. We get off at the stop and survey the territory.

"No meadow," Harper says. "Just houses." Huge houses, too close together.

"No brook either. That's how they named it."

"What?" Harper asks.

"They named it for what *was* here, what they wiped out to build it." This idea just occurred to me and seems maybe brilliant, but Harper only nods.

"See," I go on, "they could call it Oakwood if they cut down all the trees or Rolling Grove if they leveled it."

"Abby!" Harper groans. "You better hope they call us Girl Scouts. Now let's get started."

We take off the raincoats, fold and stow them, then put on our berets.

"I sure feel stupid," Harper says. "If I look as funny as you do . . ."

I adjust my badge sash over my straining buttons.

"Anything for the hurricane victims," I declare, and we head down the street.

"What are we going to tell them?" Harper asks as we turn up a brick walk. This first house is what my dad calls French Barnyard—lots of dormer windows and as much black roof as bricks.

"I've worked it out," I tell her. "Let me do this one, and you'll do the next."

I reach in my pack and take out the donation can I fixed last night. On the side I wrote *Hurricane Relief* in mock calligraphy. I even drew the Girl Scout emblem.

"Very resourceful," Harper says. "Let's see if it works."

I press the lighted doorbell.

We wait.

A kid comes to the door. A boy, maybe seven.

"Girl Scouts," he observes, then yells, "Mom! Cookies!"

So his mom comes to the door with her pocketbook in hand.

"Sorry," I say. "This isn't cookie season."

"I didn't think so," she says with a tired smile.

"We're not asking you to help *us* this time," I explain. "We're collecting money for the hurricane victims. We need you to help them."

"Just a minute," she says, and walks away.

Her hair is long, brown, and pulled back in a ponytail. Her eyes are the blue of bleached jeans.

All of her looks worn, while the house is so new, I expect to find a price tag tucked behind the bushes.

She comes back, opens the storm door a fraction, and hands us a check. *Girl Scouts of America*, it says. *Fifty dollars*.

Harper and I look at each other. We hadn't thought about checks. I don't know what to do.

"Thank you very much," I say, taking the check and folding it to fit in the slot. "That's really generous."

She smiles.

"Sorry we don't have cookies," Harper tells her.

"Come back in the spring," the faded mom offers.

"Yes, yes," we both say, backing away.

On down the sidewalk Harper announces, "Well, we blew that one. Fifty useless dollars. Now what do we do?"

"What was wrong with that woman?" I ask.

"You mean that she gave us money?"

"No. She just looked—I don't know, stunned or something."

"What has that got to do with us?"

"Don't you feel kind of drawn in? I mean, they

open their front door, and their life sort of leaks out. Don't you wonder what's going on in there?"

Harper bops me on the head. "I wonder what's going on *out here*. Abby, will you forget those people and figure out what we're going to do? We can't take another check."

I can see she's right. "Do you have any glue?" I ask. "Or tape?"

"Tape," she says, unzipping the pocket of her pack and digging it out.

I peel the sign off the coffee can. Getting a book to bear on and a pen, I write on the back of the paper:

DOLLARS AND DIMES
FOR THOSE IN HARD TIMES

HELP HURRICANE VICTIMS!!

Then I tape it back on.

"Wow!" Harper says.

"I should have thought of that in the first place."

In an hour and a half we collect fifty-seven dollars and eighty-six cents. Then we have to get home. It's almost five o'clock, and we've stretched the chorus excuse as far as it will go.

Back on the bus Harper says, "Just think, if we

really had that other fifty dollars—we'd have over a hundred!"

"Yeah, but you know what?" I ask. I've been considering this. "I think that woman was suspicious of us, and that's why she wrote a check. She didn't want to give us cash."

"Um," Harper says.

This trip we have to get a transfer, since we're going all the way home. At the downtown station we run in the bathroom and change back into school clothes. It's harder to do here than at school. I hate to put anything on the floor. The Lysol smell is so strong, it hurts my nose, but everything still looks dirty, and there are no hooks on the doors. We get adjoining stalls and drape clothes over the top. Then the bathroom door creaks open, and something rolls in—cleaning cart? Wheelchair?

"What are y'all up to in there?" a woman calls out.

"Just changing clothes," Harper answers.

"This ain't a hotel!" the voice calls back. "No bathing, no setting up residence. Soon as you get those clothes on your backs, you skedaddle, hear?"

"Yes, ma'am," I say, shuddering at the thought

that somebody might try to live here. Then I consider what's good about it: it's warm, dry. Well, most of it . . .

"Come on!" Harper calls. We get out fast.

On the ride home, she produces a granola bar from her backpack, gives me half, then says, "We squeaked by this time. What next?"

I grin at her. We may have been mistaken for con artists and bag ladies, but Harper's not about to give up now.

"Tomorrow afternoon we get the supplies," I say. "Friday we go."

"Are you serious? We can't go all that way after school."

"We won't go to school."

"Abby—"

"Look, Harper, I know it's scary to skip school, but we've *got* to if we're going to help her. And we've got to do it in a hurry. People are dying."

Harper raises her eyebrows.

"I know that sounds crazy."

She closes her eyes.

"Look," I say, and she does. "Let's take it step-by-step. We'll get the supplies together tomorrow, and maybe on Friday I'll go by myself."

"No!" she protests. "We're in this together."

"In *this* part," I say, "but maybe not the Eliza part. Maybe with her I'm supposed to be by myself."

I say this just so Harper will give me room to think, but as we walk up the bus aisle and climb down the steps, I have an awful feeling that it's true.

"Well, I don't like it," Harper says. Her face is shut tight. We trudge along in silence. Then she relents. "I've got twenty dollars saved up that I can put with what we've collected," she offers.

"And I'll put in my last two allowances. That gets us up to eighty-seven dollars." I'm wishing I hadn't bought a tape last Friday to listen to on the way to Camp Robinson.

"See you," Harper says when we come to her corner.

Usually we call back and forth till she's halfway down the street. Today we've used up our words.

"Yeah," I say, and walk on.

EIGHT

AFTER SUPPER, I sit at my desk, everything still back-to-school neat. I can't concentrate on my homework, though. Nothing adds up in math, nothing boils down in science. Spanish is like a foreign language (ha!). I think about the coffee can, heavy with money.

Heavy as my heart.

It's not me that thinks that.

Though I'm wide awake, though it's still light outside, Eliza is here. I can't deal with that. I grab my bathrobe and go take a shower.

I want water and soap to calm me down and make things clear. They don't. *Soap and water could save lives.* I hear the front door open as I'm drying off.

"I'm home," Mom tells the air. She's been to yoga.

I hear her walk down the hall and into the kitchen. By the time I'm back in my room, she clicks the microwave open.

I pull on sweat shorts and shirt, tie my running shoes tight, and head for the TV. I meet Mom in the hall.

"If you're going for a run, do it now," she says. "I don't want you out after dark."

"Yes, Mom," I say, and slip out the front door. Was I going for a run? No, I put this on because I felt antsy. I just wanted to be ready to take off.

But now that I'm out here, I might as well try a few loops. Might calm me down. I don't want to lie awake all night, waiting for Eliza. If she's coming, I wish she'd come on. No, I don't! Why did I think that?

I finish stretching and ease into a run. It must be about eight o'clock. House lights are on. The trees, still green and full, seem more important than the houses. They brood in the dimming light. Faster now, I run by the Eliotts', leap a tricycle in the McFargues' driveway, detour into the street to accommodate a moving van at the Cowleys'. Where are they going? Who will live there next? Will the house stand empty?

I'll never sleep in an empty house again, I decide, jogging in place while a radio-shaken car rolls through the intersection. I won't wear other people's clothes, won't be in plays—not historical ones anyway.

It's uphill now and I'm sweating, waving to the Clifford kids, who are catching lightning bugs in their front yard. Kendra, the middle one, is in a wheelchair, so she has the jar, and the other two run and leap and fall down laughing around her. What must it be like . . . ?

But no, there I go. I have to put myself on a leash. I can't go chasing everybody else's life. I don't have to right now anyway. There's somebody chasing me.

And she doesn't get out of breath, I think, stumbling as my right foot lands on the slope to the storm drain.

Yes, I do, Eliza tells me. *Not in this fashion, running like a colt.* I slow down. *More like a mule. Carrying water, iron kettles, wet clothes. Lifting the dead.*

I walk. Day is done. The sky Union blue. The trees outlined in ink or dried blood. All the way home I listen, but Eliza says nothing else. She's quiet enough for us both.

Mom and Dad are watching a movie. I take

another shower. I try homework again. Eat some popcorn. Watch the news. Everything seems very unlikely. I'm grateful for the solid couch. The family room. Mom and Dad. I'm glad they say the same things as always when they head up to bed: ". . . not too late, check the lights, the cat, the door."

I SIT ON the brown and green-gold couch after they've gone, admiring its indentations, its wear. One of its arms used to be my pony. I'd fasten a belt to the wooden knob for a bridle, take a towel for a saddle, and ride like the wind.

I remember a Saturday, sitting here reading *Black Beauty*—I was maybe eight—and Mom had to go to the grocery. I was so caught up in the story that she let me stay, for the first time, by myself. The way Mom tells it, when she came back, I was right where she'd left me, enthralled by the pages, but I was eating oats. By the handful, raw, right out of the Quaker Oats cylinder. The step stool was by the cabinet, but I didn't remember getting up there. Mom didn't laugh, just brought me a glass of apple juice.

"Those look kind of dry," she said.

And I said, "Horses like apples."

Which is a good story and true. But that was being a kid. This is something else.

And I'm worn out with it, I realize all of a sudden. It's almost midnight. So I follow the closing-up routine, go upstairs, and get ready for bed. But just as I'm about to pull back the covers, I decide to see if Eliza wants to write. Better now than the middle of the night.

So I sit at the desk. I open the diary and read her words. I lift the coffee can and feel the weight of her heart. Nothing comes. Is it because I'm waiting? It's not fair! I get cold, I get sleepy, maybe scribble a few words like I do when I fall asleep in class. Sometime in the night the clock downstairs strikes and startles me awake. This is ridiculous. I get up, stretch to get the kinks out of my back, and go to bed.

NINE

COME MORNING I AM UP, dressed, and loading my backpack before I even look at the diary. I expect to see the scrawl of sleep across the page. What I find is this:

I am told there will be a great battle nearby soon. Now that Nelson has lost Richmond and the Union line is back at the Ohio, Bragg is pressing for Kentucky. It will take blood to secure the Union's hold on this state: human sacrifice. "Father Abraham" they call Mr. Lincoln. Does God then demand all our Isaacs? What thicket hides the ram to offer instead?

I fear there is none, no dumb beast. Only sons and brothers, fathers, husbands. Their bones and breath, their most private flesh. As the stories stir and flags ripple in anticipation, I want to run screaming between the tents, to saddle a horse and shout through the streets of Lexington: "No more slaughter! Let us break our weapons, our mold of mind. God in heaven, give us courage to sacrifice something besides our children!"

My heart is pounding fast and loud. My glasses fog with tears.

"Abby!" Mom shouts up the stairway. "Do you want cereal or a bagel?"

Peace is the answer. I want peace. But I don't say that.

"Bagel, please," I call back.

Bagel sounds like *battle*. The Bagel of Gettysburg. I start to giggle. Don't lose it, I tell myself, but the words keep coming. The Bagel of Perryville.

Wait a minute—that was in Kentucky! Is that what Eliza's talking about?

I grab my school gear and run downstairs.

"Cream cheese or butter?" Mom asks as I slide into my place at the table.

"Butter. Mom"—she's hunting for the butter dish in the fridge—"when was the Battle of Perryville?"

"October eighth, 1862," she says, quick, as if I'd asked a phone number. "A Wednesday."

"The second year of the war?"

"Yes." She unplugs the toaster and pries out the bagel with a knife.

"A year after Camp Robinson?" I ask.

"Thirteen months," she answers.

And this is Thursday, I think, sipping orange juice, opening the honey jar. I don't know how fast time is going in the past. Maybe Perryville hasn't happened.

"Did people know the battle was coming?"

"They knew it was likely," Mom says. "The Battle of Richmond, in August, had been a big Confederate victory—"

"Richmond, Virginia?"

"No, *our* Richmond, just down the road. Bragg was pressing for Kentucky. The Federals had to take another stand."

I feel the goose bumps tingle along my arms. *Bragg was pressing for Kentucky*—those are Eliza's words!

"The newspapers were full of it," Mom goes on. "They tried to install a Confederate governor in Frankfort. Anyone who could read would have had to know a crisis was coming."

"Also where it would happen?"

"Not exactly. Just that it would be soon."

I nod. Mom pours herself more coffee and sits down.

"What's got you to thinking about Perryville?" she asks.

"Oh, the weekend," I tell her. "It kind of makes me wonder about the rest of the story." This is like saying the living room is stuffy when the couch is on fire.

"That's great!" she says. "I thought you might come around."

TEN

Wound up with the momentum of yesterday, this day moves fast. It seems like no time from the first bell till the last one, till Harper and I walk to the bus stop. Today we're headed downtown so we have to wait longer for the right bus.

"What will we get?" Harper asks.

"We'll have to see how the money goes," I tell her. "But I was thinking maybe we could get by with one duffel bag for the drugstore stuff and wrap the rest in blanket rolls."

"We're going to look pretty strange," Harper announces.

I nod.

"That hasn't stopped us yet," she says.

We smile. Yesterday we would have laughed, but we're not so lighthearted now. Maybe it was partly being disguised as Girl Scouts, our old selves. Yesterday was sunny, too, and today's all gloomy. The sky looks like dryer lint.

"This is our stop," Harper says. "Broadway and Main."

Off we get.

We have to cross the street to reach the drugstore, one of those discount kinds that's all loud signs and wire hampers. Once we're in and making our way to the first-aid section, Harper says, "This is the weirdest thing you've thought up yet, Abby."

"Thought up?" I can't believe she said that.

Harper ignores me. "Here are the bandages," she says.

I am getting furious. "Eliza is preparing for a great battle—probably Perryville—and you believe I'm making this up?"

"Do you think we should get Bactine?" Harper's freckled face and green eyes infuriate me.

"Will you listen? This is *real*! I can't help it if it doesn't make sense. . . ." I can hear my voice getting louder, climbing right up the ladder to tears, when Harper puts her hands on my shoulders.

"Cool it," she orders, "or we'll have a grownup over here to investigate. If it's war, it doesn't matter when it is. There's always going to be a battle."

I blink and breathe, blink and breathe.

Harper's looking hard at me, the corners of her thin mouth itching to smile. "On my honor as a Girl Scout," she says, "I wasn't making fun of you. It just seems hard enough to get this stuff to the past"—I nod—"without having to throw it on a moving train."

"Train?"

"I just mean it's *like* a train because it's moving."

"Sure," I say. "I'm okay now. Let's see what we've got here."

And I stare at the shelves of gauze pads, rolled bandage, adhesive tape, Band-Aids, antiseptic cream. There's so much to choose from! If only I could bring Eliza here. . . . Then a thought hits me.

"Harper, what if she can't take things they didn't have then?"

"Like what?"

"Antibiotic cream, peroxide—lots of stuff."

"Why couldn't she?"

"I don't know exactly. It just struck me that maybe there were things that wouldn't go through."

"Go through what?" she asks. I almost envy her being so dense. There's a kind of freedom in it. But I need her to understand.

"Harper, stop being so literal! Go through whatever there is to go through!"

Now it's her turn to lose it. She starts laughing. It's a giggle at first, but it gets bigger and faster. I don't want people to start staring at us, so I take her arm and we weave back through the aisles and outside. I watch the four lanes of traffic on Main Street while she gets over her fit.

"We're . . . we're weirding out!" she sputters.

"Yep."

"It's just that it's so—" She starts laughing again.

"Don't try to explain it. Forget about it," I tell her. "We're taking too long with this. We've got to buy what we need and go home."

She nods, getting quieter.

"And we won't worry about the next part."

"Okay," she says.

When we're back in the store, I pick up a red plastic basket and fill it with what's on my list: gauze pads, gauze rolls, rubbing alcohol, antibiotic cream, cotton balls, aspirin.

I see a big bottle of Betadine, an antiseptic I recognize from when Dad tore his arm on barbed wire and had to have stitches.

"What about this?" I ask Harper. "They use it to sterilize wounds."

"Sounds good to me. Would Eliza know what to do with it?"

"It's got directions," I tell her, and put it in the basket.

Saying *wounds* makes me see the boxes in the basket differently. These bandages are for accidents—scraping a knee, falling on glass—not for gunshot wounds. I feel stupid and embarrassed. I'm sorry, I tell Eliza in my head. It's so little.

A cup of water can save a life.

Faster than telegraph this comes to me, faster than fax.

Okay, I reply in the same unheard, unseen way.

"Abby!" Harper says, poking me in the ribs. "You said we should hurry. Don't stand there with your eyes closed!"

"Tweezers," I say, "small and large, and toothbrushes, toothpaste. Cough syrup and some medicine to stop diarrhea. That's one of the main things soldiers died of."

"The runs?"

"Yeah. Tennessee quickstep they called it."

I get five packages of something designed to stop your system like a truck. I have to move boxes around to get it in the basket, now piled high.

"We better quit," Harper says. "That stuff's expensive, you know. After we pay for it, a duffel bag may be all we can afford."

"You're right," I tell her, and we walk to the checkout. It occurs to me that the cashier may ask what we're going to do with so much first-aid gear and we will have no answer, but she doesn't. She looks at our purchases and at us as if she can't quite bring us into focus. Only the cash register and the money are real.

The total is over fifty dollars! I start to panic, but Harper motions me on through the line and out the door.

"These supplies are the most important," she says as we stand in the middle of the sidewalk, breaking the flow of men in business suits, women in dress-for-success. "Let's spend the rest on a duffel bag and however many blankets we can pay for."

"You're getting into this!" I say as we wait for

the light to change. A hot wind picks up grit from the street, rattles our plastic bags.

"I'm into getting home by five-thirty," she corrects me. "Mom wasn't happy when I said I'd be late again today."

"It didn't go over big at my house either."

It's hard to talk with trucks roaring by. We cross the street, walk half a block to the army surplus store, open a tall narrow door, and step in.

Where the discount drugstore was all glare and cheap color, this place is dim and drab. Also we've gone from plastic and glass to rough cloth and metal. And everything looks heavy.

"Reminds me of the hunting supply store my dad goes to," Harper says.

"No wonder," I say, and give her a significant look.

But it's wasted.

"They're alike," I tell her. "Hunting deer, hunting men . . ."

"Ugh!" she says, and shakes herself as if the thought were water she could shed. She's inspecting something on the bottom shelf.

"Hunters wear uniforms, too," I go on.

Harper swings up to face me.

"All right, Abby, that's enough! I get what you're saying. Now leave it alone! That's the trouble with you. You won't let anything go."

I try to speak, but Harper charges on.

"You have to make something out of it. Like that woman who gave us the check. You wouldn't leave her alone, wouldn't let her be. You have to *imagine* all the time. . . ."

She says *imagine* as if it were slime. She goes on waving the arms of her words, but I don't hear her. I'm dizzy, and the dull olive and khaki of the shelves around us is spurred with bits of light. Why *don't* I let things alone? What's wrong with my skin that it doesn't shut other lives out?

Harper's voice is like a radio station someone is gradually tuning in: buzz, then intonation, then word lumps, then: "I worry about you, Abby. I really do. You have to drag your whole self through everything. And it wears me out. Did I say that?"

"I hear you, Harper," I answer.

A colorless man in colorless clothes appears at the end of the aisle.

"How may I help you, young ladies?"

I'm without words, but Harper doesn't skip a beat.

"Do you have army blankets?" she asks.

A smile darts across his face like a minnow in the tank at school.

"Most certainly," he says.

"How much do they cost?" I ask.

"Six dollars for the cheapest."

"And a duffel bag?" Harper asks him.

"We have those, too," he says, leading us down the aisle, snaking through a section of inflatable rafts, and arriving at the bedding. "Are you perchance going camping?"

Harper looks at me, then lifts her chin as if to say, Follow me.

"Yes," she tells him. "With our Girl Scout troop. We were elected to come for equipment but don't have much money. Can you help us spend it right?"

The colorless man's whole face transforms. He is happy. He is helpful. He is generous. The duffel bag is ten dollars, which means we can really only afford three blankets, but he throws in one extra. "Because you girls had the sense to come here and not go to Chandler's."

Chandler's is the department store that has the Girl Scout franchise.

I can't see any other customers in the place, and

the clerk takes his time checking us out. Harper talks a mile a minute—her energy has to go somewhere—and I watch them both, like a show.

Finally, loaded like pack mules with blankets and medicine, we make it out the door. We stand looking between the cars to fountains cascading in the park across the street.

"Where to next, General?" Harper asks.

"We've got to hotfoot it to the bus station," I tell her.

"What? We don't need to walk all that way! We can catch the bus for home just down the street."

"I know. But we can't take all this home. How would we explain it? Come on. There are pay lockers at the bus station, and we've got enough change to stow it all till I come back tomorrow."

"What do you mean, *I*?" Harper asks as we start up the street.

"I told you yesterday. I think maybe this is something I should do myself."

Harper looks worried and impatient at the same time.

"Come on, Abby. Don't ditch me just because I got mad—"

"It's not that," I say.

"Well, what?"

"It's just a feeling I have. Like I can't connect with Eliza if someone else is around."

"That might not be a bad thing," Harper suggests.

"Oh, no," I tell her, holding up the bags I'm carrying. "We've come this far. We've got the supplies. I can't turn my back on Eliza now."

"Okay, okay," she says, out of breath from hauling burdens, walking fast. "But you've got to be careful, Abby. Leave something here to come back to."

"What do you mean?"

"Don't forget me," she says softly as we come in sight of the bus station. Then louder, as we go through the door, "Don't forget to come back."

ELEVEN

AFTER SUPPER I call the bus station from the phone in the hall upstairs. For sixteen dollars I can get a bus that leaves at nine-thirty and gets to Lancaster at eleven. It must stop at every telephone pole. The return bus comes by Camp Robinson around three. That would work out real well, except I don't have sixteen dollars. I have forty-eight cents. Now what?

Well, I could ask my parents for an advance on my allowance, but it would have to be over three weeks' worth, and that would require some explaining. I could try to sneak it from Mom's purse or Dad's wallet, but (a) that idea gives me the creeps and (b) they might not have that much between them. So I call Harper to see if she has any ideas.

"How could we be so dumb?" Harper asks when I explain the problem.

"Practice," I tell her. She doesn't laugh.

"Do you have any family money stashed at the house? I mean, we have a big jar we put extra change in, or money Mom finds in the laundry, and when it gets full, we order pizza or something."

"Afraid not," I say. There's silence on the line while we think. "Wait a minute!" I have to work to keep my voice down. "I've got a whole sock full of silver dollars!"

"And you had us begging door-to-door?"

"See, I'm not supposed to touch them, so I forgot about them—"

"Back up, Abby. Where did they come from?"

"Birthdays. My grandmother gave me my age in silver dollars every year till she died."

"How old were you then?"

"I don't know. Nine, I think."

"That's a lot of money. And they're probably worth more than a dollar apiece. Your parents should have put them in the bank."

"Probably so, but I'm glad they haven't. Otherwise, I'd never get back to Eliza."

"Are you sure I can't go with you?" Harper asks.

"Looks like that's how it's supposed to be," I say.

"How do you know that?"

"The same way I know not to ask too many questions."

"Aren't you scared?"

"Yep."

"Then—"

"Being scared is not a reason not to do it."

I am amazed that I say that. A part of me thinks fear is the perfect reason.

"Promise me you'll call as soon as you get back."

I promise.

"Happy time travel!" she says, but her voice wavers as if she wants to be kidding but can't.

I wish she was kidding, too. I'm okay doing homework, okay showering and all, but once I'm in bed, my heart takes a dive. This is crazy. All that stuff stored at the bus station—what was I thinking of? Sneaking out of town to the Civil War? How did I get into this?

My eyes scan the ceiling as if I could read a message in the dark. I try to be logical.

I got into this by pretending . . . reenacting . . . making believe.

All right, I'll just make believe it never happened. I'll put the lid on that pen. Throw it away. I'll do it now.

I climb out of bed, turn on the desk lamp. The pen is stuck in the diary. I won't look at the pages. I close my eyes, grab the pen, and throw it in the trash. No more magic wand! I take a deep breath. But then I lean over to turn off the light, and Eliza's voice rises from the page.

You must *listen!*

I won't do it, I say. I can't.

You were sent to me, she goes on.

Not me.

The help I've been praying for.

I'm not your help, Eliza. You listen to *me*! I'm not even alive when you are. Get somebody in your own time. Don't you have sisters, cousins?

I've gone to everyone, she says. *It's not enough.*

My heart seems to get bigger. It hurts.

You came to me, she says as I switch off the light. Steady, like two heartbeats:

                  You came   to me.

So NINE-THIRTY the next morning finds me seated on the bus, the diary like a passport zipped in my backpack. I still can't believe I'm doing this.

Once we leave town, I look out the window at cows eating their daily ton of grass. They might as well rise and fly to Ireland as me "help" the past. Stupid as they look, the cows are smarter than I am. Not a one is counting on invisible wings.

As far as I know.

Which, a part of me says, is not very far.

That's the part that got me here. Riding through little towns, rolling fields. Across the bridge high above the Kentucky River, past the Indian village, past Bob's Chair Shop, to the spot where two roads meet at Camp Robinson. Hoskins Crossroads the place used to be called. It's the name of Eliza's house, too, which was first a stagecoach stop, then an inn. Then the war came. Eliza. New owners. Renters. Reenactors. Me.

As SHE PROMISED, the bus driver pulls off on the fine-graveled shoulder of the road, and I waddle down the aisle with my possessions.

"You sure you want off here?" she asks as she gives me a hand down the steps.

"This is the place," I say. "And you'll stop for me on the way back?"

We study each other. Her uniform had to be designed for a man. She's a regular-sized woman, and she looks like a sausage in it. And what does she see in me? A runaway?

"If you'll stand on the other side there and wave your hand, I'll stop," she tells me.

"Good."

"I'll be looking for you." She climbs the steps, then turns back. "Watch for traffic," she says. "And meanness."

"Okay."

The doors hiss closed. The bus lumbers onto the asphalt, then roars off. I look across the two-lane highway to the house. It looks even more dilapidated than I remember—roof sagging, white paint peeling, windowpanes broken out. It's a broad house with center porches set into the flat front upstairs and down. There's no fence or gate now, but the gateposts still stand, leaning toward each other.

I wait till no cars are in sight, then lurch across

the road. It occurs to me as I pass between the posts and start up the walk that I'm trespassing. It's illegal, what I'm doing. If they caught me, I'd have no excuse. So that's something else to be afraid of. If I was paying any attention to fear.

I DON'T HAVE SENSE enough to worry about the door being locked till I turn the handle and nothing gives. On impulse I knock, then listen for footsteps. Nothing happens, of course. A wind stirs the leaves of the big oak beside the house, and I hear a hinge creak. There must be another door!

I run as well as a pack mule can and reach the back of the house in time to see a warped screen door bang against its frame.

The wind caught it, I tell myself. This door's as locked as the front.

But it isn't.

The door behind the screen door doesn't even have a knob. I push it open.

The room I step into was a kitchen not too long ago. I mean since linoleum, because I see patches of pale blue with gray swirls beneath the dirt, sticks, and leaves that litter the floor. Was the house this dirty last weekend and I didn't notice?

But it was night then, I remind myself. And anyway, I didn't look in this part.

I walk through what may have been a dining room, half its ceiling now a pile of plaster on the floor. I go into the parlor, the room the front door leads to. This is familiar. Now, if I just look to the right . . . Sure enough, there's the hall and the stairway. That's where I need to go.

The stairway's so narrow that it takes two trips to get all the gear up. I pile it in the middle of the little room, then sit on the gritty floor, my back to the wall.

Sunlight pours in the window behind me, the window where I stood that night, looking for the parking lot. And when I turned back, I saw this room for a minute with rosy carpet and a quilt on the dark bed. . . . Now its only furnishing is dust motes that solidify the light. Dust motes and me.

Until I sit down, I don't know how tired I am, how much effort it has taken to get here. I hear myself sigh, like an old woman. Now that I've arrived, now that I've returned to Eliza's room, I'm bewildered. Where should I leave my offerings? I don't have a clue.

But I do have the diary. Maybe the clue is in there. I hunt through my backpack for the black-

and-white-spattered notebook. I take it out and leaf through, expecting to be drawn to what I should read. Instead, a blank page dazzles me. My heart beats in my fingers. I find a pen.

I don't know how long I write, but when I'm finished, sleep sweeps over me. I stretch out on the light-struck floor and dream.

TWELVE

"TELL COLONEL POORMAN we've got to have more bandages. Today! Send anyone who can ride to Lancaster and let him go door-to-door asking for bed sheets. I've torn up more than this house can spare."

Someone mumbles an answer.

"I know that! But tell him a great battle is coming. Soon. In our fair state. I don't know where precisely. But I know I can't stop the flow of the Red Sea with a pocket handkerchief!"

I JERK AWAKE, Eliza's voice still an echo and my heart racing. Have I missed the bus? How long was I asleep? My watch says only twenty minutes. Whew! I can't believe I did that!

But now that I'm awake, I still don't know what

to do. This is ridiculous. I should be in music class. I'm going to get in big trouble, and even *I* wouldn't fall for my excuse.

All this is going around and around in my head when I hear the screak of the back door—oh, my God!—and footsteps. I want to hide, but there's no bed to get under, no closet. The window's too high to jump from.

He's coming up the stairs. I can tell by the weight and the pace it's a man, by his boot-steps. . . .

I close my eyes. But that's all. Otherwise I don't move.

He opens the door just a little.

"Miss Eliza?" he calls. Then, from the sound of it, he pushes the door wider and leans in. "Miss Eliza?"

I squeeze my eyes shut, myself small. He doesn't see me?

He closes the door and goes out.

My breath has slowed so much, my ears are ringing, and I have to haul air in to get my eyes open.

Part of me wants to jump up and run after him. But I couldn't run to save my life. My arms and legs seem made of sand. I feel about a hundred years old. A hundred and thirty. A hundred and sixty.

And he couldn't see me!

I swear I'm alive, I'm here. Look at my khaki shorts, tan legs, white Nikes. My T-shirt is bright red. I am not invisible!

But it strikes me even as I think this: *Now* I'm not invisible, but *then* I am. Somehow for a minute I was here and *then*. It must be what happens when I write in the diary. Something slips, like the sprocket chain on my bike—or no, like the gear changing because I don't stop. I go on.

And it's very clear to me what I must do. There's a cupboard downstairs, just off the kitchen, a pantry maybe, where Eliza keeps her supplies. Now that I'm here, I know this. What I need to do is restock it, add my things to her store. She will use what she can.

Relieved, I stand up—too fast, I guess, because the house seems to tilt and spin like a carnival ride. But the dizziness passes. I gather my burdens and go downstairs, through hall, parlor, and dining room back to the kitchen. Where is this pantry? What if it's been torn out?

But no, there's a door at the end of the room, a closed door with rust around the keyhole.

I know what I'll find inside before I open it: a narrow room. Along one wall, a counter with drawers and cupboards beneath, glass-fronted cabinets above. Along the other wall, hooks. For cloaks? Brooms? I can't tell. The hooks are empty when I pull the door open, but there they are. The cupboards, too. I recognize this place.

But not the man stretched out on the floor, much smaller than the smell he gives the room, much softer than his jagged voice saying, "Well, little lady, you took your time."

THIRTEEN

"WHO ARE YOU?" I ask in a voice that sounds bolder than I've ever been.

"One of many," he answers, moving with difficulty from lying down to sitting up. He's in uniform, but the cloth is so dirty and worn, I don't realize that at first. The pants could be gray or tan; the blue of the coat's gone shiny.

"Which side?" I ask him.

"How about yourself?" he replies.

"Oh, I—I'm just a visitor," I stammer.

"Yeah, well, ain't we all?"

"Excuse me?"

He laughs, throwing his head back, opening his mouth. Inside it's pink as a cat's. Is he laughing at his wit or my confusion? I study his scraggly black hair and beard, the scar under his chin where no whiskers grow. I'm amazed at how calm

I'm feeling, how glad not to be alone, when he says, "So where's the Angel? You ain't her. You're nothing but a sprout."

My heart gives a kick.

"You're looking for Eliza?"

He nods. "Come to find her special. I told her I'd come back, you see, when she wrote my name in her book. Didn't think it would take me this long. . . ."

Now it's my turn to laugh, but my throat's so tight, it comes out more like a squeak.

"Looks like a redbird but sings like a jay," the soldier says. "Why don't you set yourself down a minute? I'd stand like a gentleman and all, but I've walked a far piece, and my leg's about give out."

"Mister . . . ?"

"Lilly," he says. "Samson Lilly."

I set my stuff on the counter and the floor and sit down facing him.

"This sounds like a stupid question, I know, but . . ."

I can't seem to go on. Mr. Lilly watches me intently.

The hot little room gets hotter from my silence.

To keep from smothering, I finally say, "Mr. Lilly, are you alive?"

He laughs again, louder this time, his shoulders shaking, tears squeezed from his eyes. Still sweltering, I reach back and push open the door.

In one loud, graceless motion, Mr. Lilly lurches up and leans over me to shut it.

"There," he says, face flushed. "Let's keep our little talk private." Awkwardly, he settles back down. "Can't be too careful in an empty house." He smiles. "The folks you don't see, they're always listening."

"What folks?" My voice has a pinched sound I hate.

Mr. Lilly doesn't seem to notice.

"Travelers, little lady," he says. "Like us."

FOURTEEN

So BREATHE, I say to myself. Just breathe. And I do. It's the only sound. This room is small, but the ceiling's high. I smell the cream-colored paint. Then I notice a tiny window above Mr. Lilly's head.

"Could you open that?" I ask. "It's so hot in here."

"Don't know, but we'll give her a try," he says cheerfully.

He gets up slowly this time, leans on the counter to turn himself around, then puts the heels of his hands on the bottom of the window and pushes. Nothing.

"Painted shut," he says. "Let's see if this works."

He takes a knife out of his jacket pocket and works the blade around the frame. He pushes again. It still doesn't give.

"You could break the glass," I suggest.

"No!" He's suddenly fierce again. "I don't break things!" Then he relaxes, as if he's just thought of something. "*You* try," he says.

I have to climb up on the counter and lean awkwardly, so I can't use my full force, but it doesn't matter. The window has little resistance. I push, beat on its edges with my fist, push again, and it swings open. The breeze on my face is delicious.

"That feels good!" I say. "You must have gotten it just loose enough."

"Maybe," Mr. Lilly says. "Or maybe it depends on when it was stuck."

"What?"

"No matter. There's air. A regular spirit lifter, ain't it?"

I jump down. He grins at me a minute, then points back to the window.

"Well, look at that!" he says.

A crow hovers in our square of sky, rising and falling on the wave of wind. The sight's so strange, I can't turn away till finally the bird pivots some-how and is gone.

I turn to share this amazement with Mr. Lilly,

but he has gone, too. There is nothing where he stood before but air. My supplies are where I left them. The door is shut, the window open. I look back at a frame of perfect sky and try to slow down my heart.

Then I feel a hand on my shoulder. Light. A woman's or a child's.

I whirl around.

I SEE HER as if lit by lightning. A small woman made taller by her long dress and pinned-up hair. A high collar. Her hands, large, are lifted in front of her. Reaching out? Drawing back? She stands here beside me, all yellow-white light. Then she's gone.

Instinctively I move to where she was and hit a wall of cold air, wet as a cave's breath. It brings tears to my eyes.

"Close the window," I say out loud, my own voice startling. "Put it back like it was." I climb up on the counter again and pull the glass square shut. Instantly the room changes. Something stretched very tight lets go.

I know before my feet touch the floor I'll be able to walk to the door now. The light that was

Eliza and the chill she left behind are gone. But I can't leave yet.

Do what you came for, I remind myself, and begin opening cupboards and drawers, sorting supplies. Bottles I put in the glass-fronted cabinets; bandages, scissors, and tape in a drawer. The blankets, folded, just fit in a lower cupboard along with the duffel bag.

Once everything is stowed away, I feel relieved, and then, I don't know, gleeful somehow. We did it, Harper! I say inside. We did our part.

Then I look at my watch, panicked that I haven't thought to check the time in so long, but it's all right. It's two-twenty-five. I can leave slowly, making sure there's no sign of disturbance except what I've left in this room. I can slip out the back, then run like the wind to the front, unburdened. I can wait in the weeds or lean against the gatepost till the bus comes. The rest will be a breeze—riding to Lexington, catching the shuttle and the local bus home. Then *no more weirdness*. I'm free!

With a surge of joy I push open the pantry door, only to have it swing so freely it bangs into the kitchen wall. A redheaded, long-skirted woman is stirring something on a black stove. She looks at me.

"I'll be taking the bones out now, Miss Eliza. This broth is rich as a sick man can stomach."

"Thank you, Lannie," I hear a voice say, its motion moving in my throat.

FIFTEEN

I TURN AND LOCK the door, then smooth my skirt with the damp palms of my hands. The little room was stifling. Still I feel it is better to keep it closed up, keep out contagion, strangers. We are too many here.

No one knows for certain who is friend, who is foe. Last night this story from a boy just arrived: somewhere in the South a woman greeted the new Union camp with a basket of fried pies. Cherry, they were. Hot. Imagine the welcome! The soldier who tells this was appointed hostler that day and couldn't rush forward to accept her kindness but had to rub down and water weary beasts. He feared the pies would be gone before she reached him, and his mouth, at first juicy with hope, grew dry with disappointment. Finally, his task done, he ran to meet her.

The last two pastries lay in the cloth-lined basket, side by side like a split moon. He'd taken one sweet bite when another soldier, his cousin, ran at him, pushed the woman aside, and without a word, stuck his finger down the young man's throat.

Shock and anger hit him along with the retching, but when he lifted his head to curse, he saw his cousin doubled over at his feet. He saw his comrades writhing or dead still on the grass all around, and the woman nothing but a shawl flapping as she fled.

Each of my boys, each needs feeding. They are at my mercy, like the soldiers in that tale. I bear them *good* will, but it is only as good as my vigilance. They are sick, wounded, cannot get away. If the food is tainted, they die. Therefore, everything must be done as carefully and with as few hands as possible. Let there be no treachery.

Lannie goes with me on feeding rounds. We both spoon soup, and I talk with every soldier, taking whatever scrap of information they've given me and polishing it bright for them to see.

"Private Slone, I know your wife over in Buckhorn is thinking of you this very minute."

"Don't fret now, Mr. Caudill. Your womenfolk

will make the crop. Anybody can pick corn, pull fodder. I have done it myself."

I say this with a laugh, I, who have tended nothing but irises and roses.

"A little more, Sergeant Grayson. Just one more bite. I do believe your color is better this afternoon. Those prayers your church is praying—they are just what the Lord needs to hear."

I smile, try not to let the spoon click against his teeth. He is gray, gray, his sandy hair darkened by dirt and sweat. He is hard to feed without choking. A chest wound has caused his lungs to fill. Pray he drowns quick.

The next man, Private Lilly, is feverish, pushes Lannie's hand away. For all my bathing and changing dressings when we had them, the wound to his leg festers. I set down my bowl and spoon for a minute, take a fan from a nail on the wall and fan his face.

"As soon as I have fed everyone, I will come back to you," I promise. "New medicine has arrived this morning. It may be the very thing you need."

He half smiles without opening his eyes. "It's that," he says, "or the graveyard."

"Private Lilly," I answer, as if offended, "I do not give up that easy."

He opens one gray-green eye, keeps the other squinted in pain.

"Damned if you do," he says, and then, "Much obliged."

Then he closes his eye and lets his head sink farther into the pillow. Half a pillow it is, truth to tell. I've set Lannie to dividing what we have.

When broth has crossed the last cracked lips, I leave Lannie washing up and return to the pantry. I fill a crystal jar with ointment and carry it, along with fresh dressings, back to Private Lilly. He is sleeping loudly. His whistling breath stirs his beard like a bird in a bush. I expect him to wake when I lift the cover, but he does not, not even when I remove the dressing. His face flushes red, but through the cleaning and anointing he never wakes up.

I take this as a good sign, the sleep of recovery. Others might call it different.

So hot in here, the air heavy and still. I will sit for a minute on the porch and catch my breath. Even in these hazy harvest days, the trees keep a coolness. I will take my ease in the straight-backed chair, try my own praying.

Consider the lilies of the field. . . .

SIXTEEN

I BURST OUT of that house like a bird flung to heaven. My feet hardly hit the path. I can't think about time, can't check my watch. *I saw her. I was her.* I look with longing down the highway. A gasoline truck is coming. Then a red pickup. Then the wind.

Please, please, I'm thinking, I have to get out of here! I don't look down but move my legs to see if I'm wearing a skirt. No. And the hair in my eyes is my hair. And there's no high collar at my throat. A good thing, too. It would look pretty dumb with this T-shirt.

My head is not right, though. It feels like a balloon way above me. I'll be okay. Just don't ask me a question.

The only answer is *bus*. "Bus. Bus," I say.

"Dear bus, glorious bus." This is what Mom says when the cat won't come in at night, except the cat's name is Smidgen. And it usually doesn't work. She has to click the can opener before Smidgen appears.

That's what I need: a gas pump to flip on and off, a nozzle to rattle. "Here, bus. Best bus." I imagine it—row of pumps, hoses, the safe pavement obliterating this house—

And the bus comes. The music of its brakes, the miracle of its door.

"Been waiting long?" the driver asks, gum dancing in her mouth.

"No, not long."

"Construction down the road," she explains. "We got held up."

This strikes me as funny.

"Me, too," I say, and take a seat two rows back.

WE'RE SPEEDING over the high bridge that crosses the Kentucky. How did the soldiers cross this river? Where?

Then I see a green government sign:

CAMP NELSON NATIONAL CEMETERY

"Excuse me, but who's buried there?" I ask the driver.

"Soldiers," she says.

"Which soldiers?"

"The dead ones," says a fat man across the aisle. This gets a laugh from the first few rows.

"Civil War on up, if I'm not mistaken," the driver tells me. "I know they've got Ava Jacob's boy from Vietnam."

"It's big, then?"

She nods. "I've only been in there that once."

My mind starts rolling. If it's a national cemetery, there'll be an office, an index. It's like a phone directory; you can look people up. Maybe I could find out what happened. . . .

I'm about to yell, "Stop! I want off!" when something yanks on the balloon string and my head comes back to my shoulders. I feel my parents at home, waiting. If I jump off here, how will I get home? If I call from the cemetery, what will I tell them? I took a wrong turn walking to school? I can't scare them by not showing up, and I sure can't tell them about this.

And there's Harper, too. Harper could come with me here. This part of the trip we could take together, call it a school project.

So I distract myself, thinking about tomorrow, what I'll tell Harper, what we might do. This gets me through the bus station, the shuttle, and the ride home. What I'll do with the night I don't know.

SEVENTEEN

MOM IS MAKING OMELETS. She asks me to chop up peppers, grate cheese. I don't want to. I want to hide out in my room and try to arrive, but no such luck.

Mom tunes the radio to news while she cooks, so at least I don't have to talk. The salad is already in the refrigerator. I chop the peppers, grate the cheese, and set the table. In no time the first omelet's done. On the plate it looks like a folded yellow blanket, like a bag overpacked. I set the plate on the table and turn again to Mom. Her back, her posture at the stove, makes me think of Lannie. Where is she? Where was I?

"Abby!" Mom says. "Stop daydreaming!" She's holding out an orange plate with the second omelet. "Put this at your place and go call your dad."

Dad has fallen asleep in his recliner with the newspaper. "Dinner!" I announce, but he doesn't stir. I start to put my hand on his shoulder but hesitate. Waking my parents has always scared me. They're so vulnerable asleep, and as they struggle awake, you can see them put their armor on.

My Harper voice says, Enough already, and I put my hand on Dad's warm shoulder and give it a shake.

"Pretty exciting headlines," I say, taking the paper from his lap.

He blinks his eyes a couple of times before this registers. Finally he says, "Oh, no, it's Friday that does it."

For a few minutes after the blessing nobody says much. There's broccoli and salad to pass, there's salt and pepper. Dad's still sleepy, and I'm between worlds. Mom makes an effort at conversation.

"The repairman came to fix the dryer," she says.

"Since you got home?" Dad asks.

"No, I met him here on my lunch hour."

Mom works at the food co-op.

"What was wrong?" I ask.

"Just the switch," she says. "Thank heavens."

"Yeah," Dad muses. "Last time they replaced everything *but* the switch."

"It was still seventy-four dollars," she tells him. "And Mr. Bryant wasn't here thirty minutes."

Seventy-four dollars! That's more than we collected in an hour and a half. . . .

They have a little budget talk, then Mom asks about school. I see my chance.

"We're doing special projects in social studies," I tell her. "Genealogical research. Harper and I might go to Camp Nelson Cemetery."

"Really?" Mom asks. "Who would you be looking for?"

Sheesh. I should have been prepared for that.

"Well, not relatives to begin with," I explain. "Mr. Clayton just assigns us somebody."

"Somebody he knows is there?"

"I don't think so."

"Anybody want more broccoli? More salad?" Mom asks. No takers. "Well, I guess I'll put on some coffee while you clear the table, Abby."

"And I'll get on to yard work," Dad says. "That'll wake me up."

"Just remember," Mom tells him, "tomorrow night it's your turn to cook."

"Don't worry," he says. "I'm already soaking the hardtack."

I've got the plates scraped and rinsed and am loading the dishwasher.

"Harper and I could probably get a bus," I say, steering the conversation back where I want it to go.

"No need for that," Mom says, pouring water into the coffee maker and smiling. "Your dad and I could take you. It would be fun."

I start laughing and drop the slippery silverware. Dad comes back into the room.

"What's so funny?" he asks.

"Mom," I tell him. "She says cemeteries are fun."

Mom starts explaining, and I keep laughing, retrieving forks and knives from the floor and the bottom of the dishwasher. Finally I fish out a spoon, old and bent. It should be with Mom and Dad's Civil War gear. Just the feel of it brings back Lannie's voice, Mr. Lilly's face.

"Let's go Sunday," Dad is saying. "The weekend after, I'm tied up with work."

"Would that be good, Abby?" Mom asks. She and Dad look at me eagerly, like little kids.

They love this stuff, I think. They don't know it's real. What I say is, "I think so. I'll have to talk to Harper."

Boy, do I! But where can I begin?

Start with the bus, I think as I climb the stairs. End with the bus, I think as I punch in Harper's number. By the time she answers, I'm giggling again.

"Abby, is that you?"

"Um-hm," I answer. It's all I can get out.

"Are you all right? What are you laughing at?"

"Bus thou art, to bus returneth," I tell her, and go off on another fit.

"What?"

I forget she doesn't go to church. "It's a Bible verse," I explain.

"About buses?"

I laugh harder.

"Abby!"

"No, no, it's about *dust*. Never mind. I'm back!"

"Yeah, and I'm glad to hear it. I mean, I didn't think you'd slip through a time warp or anything, but still—"

"Well, I did."

"I still worried about you going off like that."

Silence.

Harper finally hears what I said.

"You did *what*?"

"Slipped. Went back. Saw her."

"Abby!"

"It's true. As sure as we're talking. But I'll explain that later. Right now I have a couple of questions. Are you busy Sunday?"

"No."

"Could you come with me and my parents to a cemetery for a school project?"

"What project?" she asks.

"I was hoping you'd come up with one."

HARPER AND I BIKE to the park on Saturday morning. All the little kids are watching cartoons, so it's pretty empty. As we go through the rounds of the fitness course, I tell her what happened. Last night I worked on trying to make it sound less crazy, but today I just want her to *know*. If it's crazy, that means crazy is real, too.

Harper is chinning herself when I get to the part about seeing Eliza. She lets go and drops like a cat to the ground.

"You put your hand on her?" Harper asks.

"No. She put her hand on me."

"Where?"

I point to my shoulder. Harper rests her hand there a second, then pulls back and takes off running. I follow. She circles the whole course, threads between stations, circles the course again. I keep going. Being light, Harper has always been faster than me, but I've got staying power. I'm just about to give up when she stops and stretches out under a tree. I do the same. We're breathing too hard to talk.

I can feel grass scrape the back of my neck, feel the earth wheel beneath me.

"There's more, Harper," I say finally.

She grabs my hand, gives it a squeeze, and lets go.

"Do you want to hear the rest?"

"Sure," she says, and I tell about Lannie, about feeding the soldiers, about running out of the house. I explain about the cemetery.

"Okay," she says. "I'll go. And I'll think up a project. But, Abby, promise me one thing."

"What?"

"You won't go looking for Eliza again."

"I wasn't looking for her this time!"

"No, but you know what I mean."

"Yes. And I promise. But that doesn't guarantee it's over."

"Why not?" Harper asks.

"She could still come looking for me."

EIGHTEEN

I DON'T THINK she will, though. I think the door that opened somehow is closed. All through church I think about this, worry it like a loose tooth.

Afterward, instead of driving through the Wok 'n' Go like we usually do on Sundays, we go home, eat peanut butter sandwiches, and swing by to pick up Harper. Her folks have gone to a movie, and she's waiting on the front steps, notebook in hand. She sprints to the car.

"That girl should be on the track team," Dad comments, and I remember her at the park, trying to outrun the truth.

"Pile in," Dad tells Harper. *Fold* in is more what she does.

"So who are you girls looking for?" Mom asks

us as we wind out of the subdivision and onto the bypass.

Harper looks at me for a signal.

"We'll tell you after we're done," I say. "Mr. Clayton wants us to find everything on our own, and if I tell you, it'll be hard for you not to help."

Wow! That sounded good. And I didn't even think of it, I just said it.

"I see," Mom says. "We'll wander around, then, while you do your research. We've always got friends we can visit."

"She means graves," I tell Harper.

Harper nods, then rolls her shoulders. "I'm just here for the ride," she announces.

I glare at her. I mouth *homework*.

"And for Mr. Clayton," she adds.

Whew!

By now we've almost left city traffic. Five minutes, and the road will be down to a two-lane ribbon between fields.

"So you're studying the Civil War," Dad ventures.

"Yes," Harper says at the same time I say, "No."

Everybody laughs.

"We're not yet, but we *will* be," I explain. "Now we're exploring different ways to do research. Harper's subject just happens to be a Union soldier."

"Makes sense," Dad says.

Harper looks at me as if to say, Let's hope he gets tired of questions before you run out of bluff.

As if on cue, Dad says, "Well, there's nothing like music to give you a feel for the past. And I just happen to have—"

"A tape of every song either side ever heard," Mom finishes.

"I wish," Dad says, then fishes a tape from the basket between the seats and pops it in. We hear first drums, then voices:

> We are coming, Father Abraham,
> Three hundred thousand more!

So the fields roll by and the songs spin out, about those marching bright and brave, about others alone and brokenhearted.

> We shall meet, but we shall miss him.
> There will be one vacant chair. . . .

Eliza must have known these songs, maybe heard them in Lexington at parades or listened to them sung in camp. Mr. Lilly might have been among the singers.

> The Union forever!
> Hurrah, boys, hurrah!
> Down with the traitor
> And up with the star!

I thought I might be scared going back over this road, and I worried how I'd explain the shakes, but I'm not scared really. Excited that we might find something. Nervous about what it could be.

We're almost there when the tape hits "The Battle Hymn of the Republic," which my parents feel compelled to sing. I look over at Harper for sympathy, and to my astonishment, she's singing, too. I give up and join in.

We arrive at the turnoff and the last verse at the same time, so we're passing through the wrought-iron cemetery gates as we sing:

> In the beauty of the lilies
> Christ was born across the sea.

We drive under a canopy of trees to a little parking lot. There's an office beside it. And in every direction except the one we came, the grass is ridged with white tombstones like teeth.

Does Mr. Lilly lie under one of those? If he does, who was the man at Eliza's house?

NINETEEN

OUR CAR IS LITTLE, but Dad is tall, so when he gets out he has to stretch. Today he's hot, too; sweat makes dark wings on the back of his shirt.

True to her word, Mom takes him off on their own. Both refrain from pointing me to the directory, which I find easily. It's a big notebook with plastic-covered pages on a stand in front of the office.

"Not exactly personal, is it?" says Harper, looking over my shoulder.

"Neither is the phone book," I remind her.

I flip to the *L*s. My heart rises.

> Lark
> Lenning
> Libby
> Lilly

"Look!" I say to Harper, grabbing her arm. "There he is!"

Lilly, Samson   E   2586   Pvt.

"Where's the map?" Harper says. "Come on. We've got to find *E*." She spots the roofed bulletin board across the path and dashes over there.

I can't move. *Samson Lilly*, it says. *E-2586*. He was real!

Harper is back, saying something.

I didn't make him up. He lived. He was a soldier. I found him.

"Abby!" Harper is in front of me now, head down so her forehead touches mine. "You are paralyzed and looking stricken in a public place. That's not inconspicuous."

"But, Harper, he's *dead*!"

She starts a wicked sort of giggle. "You're surprised?"

I stare at her.

"You did come looking for him in a cemetery."

I have to laugh. "Okay," I say. "Lead on."

There's a low wall around the old part of the cemetery. I follow Harper through the gate, onto the grass, and between the grave rows. Green and peaceful, just like they say. Hallowed rest. Then what was Mr. Lilly doing looking for Eliza? Who woke him up?

"Oh, God," I say.

"What is it?"

"I just—I don't know. Never mind. Keep going."

We come to the *E* section, and Harper begins counting rows. We're standing in the shade of a huge tree, so big and old it's got to have been alive back then. Mom says the roots of a tree have to be as big as its branches to support it. Like our stories grow from the stories of the dead.

I woke Mr. Lilly up, it seems to me. Or I woke Eliza, and she woke him. Or the reenactment woke Eliza—

Harper stops so quickly, I run into her.

"Here we are," she says, pointing.

I close my eyes a minute before focusing on the stone. It's government issue, white as those rocks people put under their bushes.

2586
Pvt. S. Lilly
98th Ohio Inft.
1905

A wonderful current flashes through me. 1905. He made it! Survived that wound forty years. Lived to be an old man.

Conspicuous or not, I sit down on the grave and put my head on my knees. He came back to thank Eliza, but it was *me* he found.

After a minute or two I look up and touch the stone. "Travelers, little lady," he said. "Like us."

A couple in shorts and tank tops strolls by, the man carrying a sleeping baby. He looks at me, crying on Mr. Lilly's grave.

"Just got word?" he asks.

I nod, realizing it's true.

TWENTY

"So now what?" Harper asks. The clouds could part and an angel walk toward you, and Harper would say, "So now what?"

"I—I don't know. I guess we go home," I tell her, getting to my feet, watching the world reappear.

"What does this mean?" She stands there, thin and intent. She is not shaking a foot or doing arm rotations or striding off. Harper is still. She's waiting.

"He didn't die in the war," I say.

"Did we save him?"

I look at the headstones, which don't run in straight rows, stone wall to stone wall, but make curves or meet at corners, in arrangements graceful and unlikely.

"It's impossible," I say. "But that doesn't mean it didn't happen."

"Right." Harper does not budge.

"I mean, how did I know about Mr. Lilly in the first place?"

"That's what I want to know."

"Well, I can't tell you. *Something* happened is all I can say."

Caw-caw, caw-caw! Crows rise from a cornfield outside the cemetery wall.

"If it's true, everything is different," Harper says, turns away, and heads toward the gate.

I look around for my parents. The cemetery isn't huge, but it's big enough, and the ground rolling enough, that you can't see the whole thing at once. Time could be like that: everyone, every time always there, just no place to stand so you can see. Like the ocean. But sometimes a riptide pulls you out farther, a squall blows you way off course. . . .

"Abby." Mom's voice and her hand on my arm cause me to jump about two feet. "Are you ready to go? Where's Harper?"

"In the rest room," I say. "Or back at the car."

"Did you girls find what you needed?" Dad asks.

I nod. "This is him," I say, pointing at the headstone.

"Ninety-eighth Ohio," Dad observes. "He was at Perryville."

"And lived to tell about it," Mom adds.

"Jackson's division," Dad goes on. "One of the hardest hit. Lost their commanders—Jackson, Webster, Terrill, all killed. And for your fellow's regiment"—Dad nods toward the marker—"for the Ninety-eighth Ohio, this bloodbath was the first battle. Baptized at Perryville. Lost over two hundred men."

"Harper drew a lucky one," Mom says.

It's like someone put an ice cube down my back. I shake my head and roll my shoulders.

"Mosquitoes," I say, and slap at the back of my neck. "Let's go."

I want to keep quiet as we walk toward the car. I try to lock my jaws. We pass through ripples of light and dark, under the full trees. I will keep my question till we get outside the wall. Okay. Okay. Harper's leaning against the car. I won't ask till we're all inside, till we're on the road. Doors open.

Volcano breath of the car. We get in anyway. Doors close. We leave. Everybody's hot. Nobody's talking. Go on.

"I was wondering," I begin, as casual as someone about to go over a cliff. "If Mr. Lilly was wounded at Perryville—I mean, I don't know if he was—could Eliza have taken care of him?"

"*Your* Eliza?" Mom asks.

"Who else?"

"Don't be a smart aleck, Abby," Dad says. "Miss Hoskins wasn't the only Eliza around. Why, of the commanding generals at Perryville, Bragg and Buell, one had a mother and one had a wife named Eliza. . . ."

Harper is rolling her eyes. Mom looks at me, then at Dad. "You're lecturing," she says in a stage whisper.

"Sorry."

"Okay," I say. "I mean Eliza Hoskins."

"I don't think she would have gone to Perryville."

"Could they have brought the injured to Camp Robinson?"

"I doubt it. There wasn't money or time or equipment to move them far. And you're talking twenty-plus miles. They used everything close: hospitals first, then churches, schools, hotels, and finally private houses."

"There were lots of casualties at Perryville?" Harper asks.

"Over seven thousand," Mom says.

"My God!" Harper answers.

There has to be some way, I'm thinking, some circumstance that got Mr. Lilly to Eliza, when Mom says, "Prisoners. What about prisoners? Didn't part of Bragg's army retreat that way?"

"Well, yes," Dad says, slowing down as we come up behind a tobacco truck. "Part of it went by Camp Robinson, part by Bryantsville. I suppose they could have dropped off prisoners too sick to travel. . . ."

I'm leaning toward the front seat, my heart galloping. I want to tell them everything, but what I say is, "Just think, maybe the woman whose part I played saved Harper's soldier's life."

"Whoa, now," Dad puts in. "That would be a pretty big coincidence. For that matter, I don't even see why this Lilly fellow's buried at Camp Nelson. An Ohio soldier. He didn't *die* here, unless he moved to Kentucky after the war."

"He could have requested it," Mom offered. "That happened."

"But it's rare," Dad says. "Why would he do that?"

"Maybe *because* of Eliza," I tell them. "Maybe she saved his life, and he wanted—"

"Hold on there, Abby! Your imagination is working overtime. Remember, we don't really have Eliza's story. She's come down to us more as a legend than a real person."

"That's why no one's ever portrayed her before," Mom explains.

"*What?*" I shiver. I didn't know that.

"There's so little to go on," Mom continues. "With soldiers you have documents, but there aren't any for Eliza."

Harper gives me a wild-eyed look. Should we laugh? Scream? Cry?

"Maybe they'll find some," Harper says. "You never know."

TWENTY-ONE

AFTER THAT EXCHANGE, Dad puts the tape back on. Harper and I are quiet. We can't talk in front of the grown-ups. I don't know what we'd say anyway. Evidently Harper doesn't either. When we get to her house, she springs out and says, "I've got a pile of homework, so I'd better get to it. See you tomorrow."

No discussion there.

At home I do my math, eat the ritual Sunday-night hamburger, conjugate verbs, run a mile, take a shower, do laundry, stand in the backyard and stare at the moon—anything I can think of to avoid sitting still with what's happened.

A week ago, when all this started, I tried to keep it to myself, but I couldn't. I had to tell Harper. Now I want to shut up about it. I don't want to breathe a word.

I don't even like that expression. Because that's what happened, isn't it? I breathed *her* words somehow. I put on Eliza's clothes, sat in her room, and breathed her words as though they were her smell, the dust of her skin left in the cloth. . . .

Ugh! I am not going to think about this! Whatever it is, it's over. If I went looking for Eliza a week ago, I'm not looking now.

Then why am I sitting on the bed with her diary in my hands?

Mom said there were no documents, but I have Eliza's words right here. Shouldn't somebody read them? I could put the notebook with her clothes when we give them back. . . . No, that wouldn't work. She didn't have a Rite Aid composition book. And even if I found an old blank journal to copy this in, the handwriting and ink would give me away.

Maybe when I'm grown up, somebody would believe it. Maybe by then scientists . . .

I start to get dozy, but a memory buzzes in my brain. Didn't I write something as I fell asleep at Camp Robinson, that day I met Mr. Lilly? In all that's happened since, I forgot about it. I open the diary, flip through the pages, catching phrases, holding my breath. Do I want to find something?

Whether I do or not, there it is. In my handwriting, of course, but I can see now that it's not *exactly* mine. Something is pushing the letters to a fullness, like wind in a sail.

> *I was walking home through camp last night when I heard a fiddler take up a plaintive tune. It was none I knew, yet it dragged at my heart. I had been sewing as I sat by the wounded, and perhaps that is why I felt the fiddler's bow as a needle, piercing the air, pulling down music like thread. Stitch us a wedding garment, I wanted to say, a warm coat, not a shroud. But the melody went on mournful. It knew what it knew. I looked to Heaven for comfort. The full moon hung above us, remote, perfect as peace.*

It knew what it knew. I can't *explain* this story—not to myself, not to Harper—only tell it, like the fiddle. Set it down so I won't forget. Maybe someday that will be a document.

The diary still has a few blank pages. I can begin here and get another notebook tomorrow. A special pen. Supplies.

Eliza, you'll not be forgotten. See: I have written your name.